Evelyn
the Mermicorn
Fairy

Join the **Rainbow Magic Reading Challenge!**

Read the story and collect your fairy points to climb the

For Coco, who loves mermicorns
and always speaks her mind

ORCHARD BOOKS

First published in Great Britain in 2018 by The Watts Publishing Group

1 3 5 7 9 10 8 6 4 2

© 2018 Rainbow Magic Limited.
© 2018 HIT Entertainment Limited.
Illustrations © Orchard Books 2018

A CIP catalogue record for this book is available from the British Library.

ISBN 978 1 40835 754 5

Printed and bound in Great Britain by CPI Group (UK) Ltd, Croydon, CR0 4YY

MIX
Paper from
responsible sources
FSC® C104740

The paper and board used in this book are made from wood from responsible sources

Orchard Books
An imprint of Hachette Children's Group
Part of The Watts Publishing Group Limited
Carmelite House, 50 Victoria Embankment, London EC4Y 0DZ

An Hachette UK Company
www.hachette.co.uk
www.hachettechildrens.co.uk

Summer Days at Sunrise Farm

Lucy Daniels

Veterinary nurse Helen Steer adores her job at Animal Ark, and with the summer ahead things couldn't be better.

That is until her best friend goes travelling, leaving Helen unexpectedly jealous – and questioning her own stable life with her boyfriend Seb. Charming new vet Toby Gordon, with his flirtatious wit and mysterious family background, suddenly seems a much more exciting prospect.

But just as Helen and Toby's friendship starts to become something more, Sunrise Farm, the beautiful fruit farm where Helen lives, is hit by a crisis leaving its future in the balance. Along with her friends Mandy and James, who put aside their own problems to help, Helen throws everything she has into saving her home.

Though with so much at stake, is there time to think about a new relationship? Or will Helen be forced to let her second chance at love slip away?

HODDER

Springtime at Wildacre
Lucy Daniels

Mandy Hope is on cloud nine. Hope Meadows,
the animal rescue and rehabilitation centre she founded,
is going really well. And she's growing ever closer to
handsome villager Jimmy Marsh. What's more,
James Hunter, her best friend, is slowly learning
to re-embrace life after facing tragedy.

But when an unexpected crisis causes Mandy to
lose confidence in her veterinary skills, it's a huge blow.
If she can't learn to forgive herself, then her relationship
with Jimmy, and the future of Hope Meadows, may be
in danger. It'll take friendship, love, community spirit –
and one elephant with very bad teeth – to remind
Mandy and her fellow villagers that springtime in
Yorkshire really is the most glorious time of the year.

HODDER

Evelyn
the Mermicorn
Fairy

by Daisy Meadows

ORCHARD

www.rainbowmagicbooks.co.uk

Contents

Story One:

Believing in Yourself

Story Two:

Speaking Your Mind

Story Three:

Helping Others

Jack Frost's Spell

Now Topaz makes each fairy pest
Quite confident that they know best.
But when I steal her gems so bright,
Each fairy's wisdom will take flight.

I'll make them fear and hesitate,
Until they're in an awful state.
And when they cannot give advice,
I'll cover Fairyland in ice!

Story One
Believing in Yourself

Chapter One
A Rainy Morning in Tippington

"I love listening to the rain beating on the window," said Rachel Walker. "Especially when it's so cosy inside."

She snuggled deeper into her favourite armchair and gazed into the flickering

flames of the fire. Her best friend, Kirsty Tate, put down the pattern she was stitching.

"Me too," she said.

Kirsty was spending the last week of the holidays at Rachel's house in Tippington. Although they went to different schools, they saw each other as often as they could. They always had the best fun when they were together, and they often shared secret, magical adventures with their fairy friends.

The sitting room door opened and Rachel's dad popped his head around it.

"Anyone for hot chocolate?" he asked.

"Yes please," said the girls together.

"With whipped cream and sprinkles?" Rachel added.

"Of course," said Mr Walker. "Maybe

it'll make up for not being able to go pebble collecting on the beach. What did you want the pebbles for?"

"We were going to paint inspiring pictures and messages on them, and then put them back on the beach for other people to find," Kirsty explained.

"But it's OK," said Rachel. "We found something else crafty to do instead."

Her dad looked at the cross-stitch patterns they were holding. Kirsty was working on a turquoise mermaid with golden hair, and Rachel was stitching a snow-white unicorn.

"Those look complicated," he said.

"Yes, but it'll be a great feeling when they're finished," said Kirsty.

Mr Walker went to make the hot chocolate, and the girls carried on stitching.

"What's your favourite, mermaids or unicorns?" asked Rachel.

"I don't think I can choose," said Kirsty. "After all, we've met them both on our adventures, and they were just as magical and inspiring as each other."

Just then, they heard a tiny, tinkling giggle. The girls exchanged a surprised glance.

"That sounded exactly like a fairy," said Rachel.

There was another bell-like giggle, and the girls jumped to their feet.

"Where are you?" Kirsty asked.

Then Rachel noticed that her dark

hair was sprinkled with sparkling fairy dust. Kirsty saw the same thing on Rachel's hair. They both looked up at the same time, and laughed out loud.

A chestnut-haired fairy was waving at them from the top

of the round glass light pendant. She
slid down it with a whoop and turned
somersaults through the air, landing on
the sofa arm with a bounce. She was
wearing a shimmering, glittery blue skirt
and a matching denim jacket.

"Hello," she said.
"I'm Evelyn the
Mermicorn Fairy."

"Hello, Evelyn,"
said Rachel,
kneeling down
in front of
her. "What has
brought you to my
sitting room?"

"And what's a mermicorn?" Kirsty
added.

"Exactly what it sounds like," said

Evelyn with a smile. "It's the rarest, most magical creature in all of Fairyland – half mermaid and half unicorn."

"Oh, it sounds wonderful," said Kirsty in a whisper. "I wish I could see one."

"We only see them once a year," said Evelyn. "We always celebrate their visit with the Mermicorn Festival. That's why

I'm here. Would you like to come and enjoy the festival with me?"

Rachel and Kirsty squealed in excitement.

"We'd love to," said Kirsty.

"Then it's time to go to Fairyland," said Evelyn.

Chapter Two
A Fairy Without a Wand

Evelyn opened her hand, and the girls saw that she was holding a little pile of sparkling fairy dust.

"Don't you have a wand?" asked Rachel.

Evelyn smiled.

"Not today," she said.

She blew the fairy dust towards the girls, and a pastel rainbow swirled around them. Everything shimmered in light shades of blue, yellow, green and pink. Rachel and Kirsty reached for each other's hand as their delicate wings unfolded.

"Listen," said Kirsty. "The rain sounds different."

"Yes, I can't hear the raindrops spattering against the window any more,"

said Rachel. "It sounds more like ... waves."

At that moment, the pastel-coloured swirl of fairy dust vanished away, and the girls found themselves sitting on a small stretch of golden sand.

"It *was* waves," said Kirsty in delight. "Yippee, we made to the beach after all."

"This is a bit more magical than the one I was planning to visit," said Rachel with a happy laugh.

"Welcome to Mermicorn Island," said Evelyn.

"I've never seen such fine sand," said Kirsty, letting it run through her fingers.

"Or such blue sea," Rachel added, cartwheeling down to the shore.

The sun was sparkling on the water, and it looked as if tiny diamonds were dancing in the waves. As Rachel turned around to smile at her best friend, she saw a beautiful sight. At the edge of the beach was a row of candy-coloured stalls, gleaming with a pearly sheen. Fairies were walking barefoot from stall to stall, wearing shells plaited into their hair and pearls threaded into necklaces and

belts. The Music Fairies were playing an oceanic tune on driftwood instruments.

"I can taste the salt in the air," said Kirsty, taking a deep breath.

"What happens at the Mermicorn Festival?" Rachel asked.

"Music, dancing, good food, good fun," said Evelyn, spinning around with her arms held wide. "It's my favourite time of year."

Just then, Shannon the Ocean Fairy came dancing across the sand towards them.

"Rachel and Kirsty!" she cried, giving them a hug. "It's great to see you. Evelyn, when will the mermicorns be here? I can't wait to see them."

"Very soon," said Evelyn. "Let's get everyone to come down to the shore."

"Why is everyone walking?" asked

Rachel, as they watched their fairy
friends moving down to the shore.

"Because even fairies like to feel the
sand between our toes sometimes," said
Evelyn, smiling. "We all leave our wands
at the palace when we come here. We
agreed that Mermicorn Island should
only be for Mermicorn magic."

Just then, the music changed. It was

as gentle and flowing as the waves.
The shallow, clear water began to swirl
around in a whirlpool.

"Wow, the water's changing colour,"
said Kirsty.

The whirlpool had turned a lighter,
more sparkling blue, and seemed to be lit
by a light from below.

"Something's coming out of it," said
Rachel, tingling all over with excitement.

Chapter Three
Whirlpool Magic

Rachel and Kirsty watched as a spiral horn rose up through the swirling water. The head and neck of a beautiful unicorn appeared. Three colourful gemstones hung around her neck on a golden chain. Then a sparkling green mermaid tail flicked out of the water.

The fairies cheered and waved, and the mermicorn bowed its head. Evelyn waded out to the whirlpool and reached out her hand.

"This is Topaz," said Evelyn.

She let her hand rest on Topaz's mane for a moment. Rachel and Kirsty followed Evelyn and did the same thing, and at once a strong feeling of

confidence flooded through them. At the same time, the gems Topaz was wearing glowed even more brightly.

"How funny," said Kirsty. "I've been feeling worried about the homework project I chose to do for school, but all of a sudden I feel certain that I picked the right one."

Evelyn smiled.

"Topaz's magic is working," she said. "You see, the gems that she wears have the power to make everyone around them feel confident. Her blue gem gives you confidence in your own choices and ideas. Her pink gem gives you confidence to speak your mind, and helps you be brave enough to stand up for the things you believe in. And the green gem gives you the confidence to advise others."

Just then, several other mermicorns
broke through the foaming waters, each
with a different-coloured tail. The other
fairies were all in the water now, and
they started to play with the mermicorns,
stroking their manes, laughing and
singing. The mermicorns were leaping

through the foamy waves, flicking their tails. Topaz stayed close to Evelyn, nuzzling close, with love in her big, shining eyes.

"What an amazing sight," said Rachel, looking around in wonder at the fairies and mermicorns.

"This festival gives us confidence and energy every year," said Evelyn. "And the mermicorns love spending time with the fairies. We've planned a feast on the beach for later, and a dance under the moonlight. This is going to be the best festival yet."

"WRONG!" yelled a rasping voice.

There was a loud roar, and something came hurtling through the water towards the fairies and the mermicorns.

"A speedboat!" cried Rachel.

The boat turned hard in the waves, sending a wall of water crashing over the fairies. There were three goblins in the back of the boat, and everyone recognised the driver.

"Jack Frost," said Kirsty. "We should have guessed."

"Get her!" shouted Jack Frost.

Cackling with laughter, the goblins threw an ice-blue net over Topaz.

"You can't catch a magical mermicorn with a fishing net," said Evelyn, fluttering her wings. "It can't hold her."

"This isn't an ordinary net," said Jack Frost with a sneer. "Besides, it's not your silly mermicorn I want. I heard a rumour that her gems give confidence. Now I know why you pesky fairies are always thinking you know best. Without the gems, you'll never be confident enough to stand up to me!"

"Stop!" cried Kirsty. "You wouldn't dare take them when you're surrounded by fairies."

"Fairies without their wands," scoffed Jack Frost. "You can't stop me!"

He tugged on the net, and it snapped back into his hand. The little mermicorn let out a cry of shock and misery. Then Jack Frost held up the three gems.

"My magical net catches whatever I want," he gloated. "And I want these."

There was a flash of blue light and a crack of thunder, and the speedboat disappeared, taking Jack Frost and the magical gems with it.

Chapter Four
All at Sea

The mermicorns gathered around Topaz and Evelyn, looking frightened and unhappy. Evelyn put her arms out to try to stroke them all.

"What are we going to do?" she asked.

The other fairies made a circle around the mermicorns.

"I think we should go and get our wands," said Shannon.

"First we should tell the king and queen what's happened," said Victoria the Violin Fairy.

They exchanged a worried glance.

"Maybe you're right," said Shannon in a shaky voice.

"No, maybe your idea is better," said
Victoria.

Rachel and Kirsty looked around. All
the fairies started talking at once, sharing
their ideas. But no one felt sure which
idea was best. At last, Evelyn rose out of
the water and fluttered above everyone.

"It's hard to have the confidence to
decide, because Topaz's gems are missing,"
she said. "We have to get them back."

"Maybe we should ask the king and
queen what to do," called Daisy the
Festival Fairy.

The fairies murmured and nodded, and
then shrugged their shoulders and stared
at each other. No one felt confident
enough to make a choice.

Kirsty felt unsure too. But then she
remembered that her best friend always

made her feel stronger. She took Rachel's hand, and a little bit of confidence flickered inside her.

"Let me and Rachel try to rescue the gems," she said.

"Not without me," said Evelyn.

"Shall the rest of us go back to the Fairyland Palace?" asked Victoria.

She didn't sound very sure, but Rachel and Kirsty nodded, and the fairies hugged them goodbye and flew away.

"Let's fly towards the Ice Castle," said Kirsty, still holding tightly to Rachel's hand. "Maybe we will have a better idea on the way."

Evelyn came over and the three friends held hands. Instantly they all felt a little bit more confident.

"Topaz, go home to Mermicorn City," said Evelyn. "You'll be safe there until we can find your gems."

Topaz turned to the other mermicorns and made a few gentle whinnying sounds. At once, the mermicorns dived under the waves with a flick of their bright tails. But Topaz did not join them. She looked at Evelyn and shook her head.

"She won't go home without her gems," said Evelyn. "All right, Topaz, I understand. Maybe you can help us search."

Feeling unsure of where to start looking, the fairies rose up and started to fly. Topaz swam below them, leaping through the waves. They had not gone far before the mermicorn let out a high-pitched whinny, and speeded up.

"She's seen something," said Evelyn.
"Come on!"

Topaz was already ahead of them. She
was streaking through the water towards
a little boat in the distance.

"Is that the speedboat?" asked Evelyn.

"No," said Kirsty. "It looks like a rowing
boat."

"There are two people in it," said
Rachel in an excited voice. "I think
they're green."

The three fairies reached the little red
boat bobbing on the water and hovered
above it. Sure enough, two grumpy-faced
goblins were squatting inside.

"What shall we do?" asked Evelyn. "I
can't decide."

Topaz was swimming around the boat,
and the goblins were yelling at her.

"Go away!"

"Leave us alone, you big goldfish!"

Rachel zoomed down and perched on the side of the boat. Kirsty and Evelyn landed beside her. At once, Topaz's velvety head rose out of the water. She was glaring at the bigger goblin, and Evelyn gasped.

"Look at his hand," she said.

The goblin had something clutched in his fist. He was trying to hide it, but a bright blue light was shining through his closed fingers.

"The blue gem," said Rachel. "We've found it."

Chapter Five
Topaz to the Rescue

"Give Topaz's gem back," said Kirsty.

But the goblin just blew a raspberry at her and dropped the gem back in his pocket.

"What are we going to do?" asked Evelyn. "I don't have my wand, so we can't use magic to help us."

Kirsty had an idea.

"Goblins, do you enjoy being out here on the boat by yourselves?" she asked.

The goblins shook their heads.

"It's boring," said one.

"I'm hungry," said the other.

"If you give us the gem, you'll be able to go home," said Kirsty. "You won't need to guard anything."

"We'd need to guard ourselves against
Jack Frost," said the bigger goblin. "Go
away and leave us alone."

He waved an arm at them, and
accidentally hit the smaller goblin in the
face.

"Watch out, idiot," said the smaller
goblin.

The bigger goblin poked his shoulder
with one long, bony finger. The smaller
goblin gave him a shove.

"Stop squabbling," said Rachel.

But the goblins took no notice. They
stood up and jostled each other. The
bigger goblin stamped on the smaller
goblin's toes.

"YOWCH!" he yelled, hopping around
on one leg.

He lost his balance and fell sideways.

SPLASH! He sent the bigger goblin straight over the side of the boat and into the water!

"Help!" gurgled the bigger goblin. "Help! I can't swim!"

Evelyn was about to help, but Kirsty stopped her.

"Wait," she said. "Look. Maybe this time, we need to give the mermicorn magic a chance."

Topaz dived under the goblin, and suddenly he was riding a mermicorn! A happy smile spread over his face. He leaned forward and pressed his face into Topaz's mane. He cuddled her and  stroked her soft skin. Then he reached into his pocket and put the blue gem back around her neck.

"Thank you for saving me," he whispered.

Rachel and Kirsty were astonished.

They had never seen a goblin be so gentle.

"Perhaps it's the mermicorn magic," said Rachel in a whisper. "It made me feel wonderful when I stroked Topaz before. Maybe it's making the goblin feel like doing the right thing."

The goblin climbed back into the boat, and the fairies fluttered over to join Topaz. As the goblins rowed away, Topaz nuzzled each of the fairies. Evelyn threw her arms around Rachel and Kirsty.

"Thank you for being with me today," she said. "Without your help, I would never have found the blue gem."

"You're welcome," said Kirsty. "I just hope that we can help you to find the

other gems soon."

"Me too," said Evelyn. "Without them, people and fairies will lose their confidence."

"Let's go and get your wand back," said Kirsty. "Then we can start making a plan to find the gems."

Rachel smiled at her.

"It's great to hear you sounding confident again," she said. "Race you to the Fairyland Palace!"

Story Two
Speaking Your Mind

Chapter Six
Jack Frost's Magical Snowflake

The towers of the pink Fairyland Palace glimmered in the sunshine. Rachel, Kirsty and Evelyn fluttered down and landed on the polished steps. At once, the doors were flung open. Bertram the frog footman bowed and smiled at them.

"Her Majesty Queen Titania is waiting

for you at the Seeing Pool," he said.

"Thanks, Bertram," said Rachel. "It's great to see you again!"

The fairies zoomed around the palace to the gardens. They swooped under an archway of roses and landed beside the sparkling Seeing Pool. They had been here many times before, but they had never seen so many fairies gathered around the shining water.

"It looks as if everyone from the festival is here," said Kirsty.

Queen Titania was standing among the fairies. Rachel, Kirsty and Evelyn curtsied to her.

"I knew that you would come," she said.

"We got Topaz's blue gem back, thanks to Rachel and Kirsty," said Evelyn.

"But Jack Frost still has the other two gems," said Kirsty. "Without them, people and fairies are going to lose the confidence to speak their minds and give advice."

"We must find the gems," Rachel said.

"Let's find out what the Seeing Pool

can tell us," said the queen.

She held her wand out over the water, and at once a picture appeared. It was as clear as a reflection in a mirror. Jack Frost was standing over a young goblin, clutching Topaz's pink gemstone in his hand.

"Take this to the goblin village and hide it," he said.

The goblin, who was wearing a woolly hat and sparkly orange sandals, snatched the gemstone. He threw it up into the air and caught it again, squawking with laughter.

"Do you think this is a joke?" snarled Jack Frost. "Those fairies will try all sorts of tricky things to get that gem."

"I'll hide it," the goblin promised, puffing out his chest. "Those sneaky fairies can't trick me."

"Of course they can, banana brain," Jack Frost sneered. "But I'm going to give you something that will stop them."

He pulled something small and blue from his cloak. It twinkled in the daylight, and the goblin gasped.

"I love it," he said. "What is it?"

"It's a magical snowflake," said Jack Frost. "If any fairies bother you, just

throw this at them. It'll turn into a net
and send them straight to the Ice Castle
dungeons."

"You're a genius," said the goblin,
staring at Jack Frost in awe.

Jack Frost threw back his spiky head
and cackled with delight. Then the
water of the Seeing Pool rippled, and the
picture faded away.

Queen Titania
turned to the fairies
with a serious
expression.

"With the
magical snowflake,
the goblin can send
any fairy to the
Ice Castle dungeon,"
she said. "It will be

dangerous and difficult to get the pink gemstone."

"I don't care how dangerous it is," said Evelyn. "Topaz and the other mermicorns are depending on me to help them. I'll go to the goblin village."

"We'll go with you," said Rachel at once. "Kirsty and I have been to Goblin Grotto before, and we might be able to help."

"Thank you," said Evelyn with a relieved smile.

The other fairies clapped and called, "Good luck!" and "Be careful!" Then Rachel, Kirsty and Evelyn curtsied to the queen and zoomed off into the blue sky. Glancing over her shoulder, Kirsty saw dozens of fairy wings glimmering and fluttering below. The queen's hand was raised as she waved goodbye.

"We can't let them down," Kirsty said fiercely. "We must get the gemstone and take it back to Topaz."

Chapter Seven
A Speech in Goblin Grotto

By the time the fairies reached Goblin
Grotto, the cold was making them shiver.
They landed in a narrow side street.
Cobbles poked through grey snow, dirty
from goblin feet. The street was lined
with the goblins' wonky huts, and icicles
hung from the eaves.

"Time for a little mermicorn magic," said Evelyn, smiling.

She reached up and broke off the biggest icicle. As soon as her wand

touched it, the icicle started to shimmer like pearl, showing all the colours of the rainbow.

"It reminds me of Topaz's horn," said Rachel.

Evelyn tapped each of them on the shoulder with the icicle. At once, they stopped feeling cold.

"It's like wearing an invisible coat," said Kirsty.

"The magic will last until the icicle melts," said Evelyn.

She attached the icicle to the eaves

again, and looked around. There wasn't a
goblin in sight.

"Where shall we start looking?" she
asked.

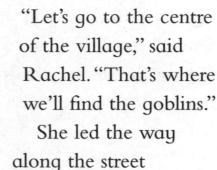

"Let's go to the centre
of the village," said
Rachel. "That's where
we'll find the goblins."
She led the way
along the street
towards the square in the
middle of the village. As they
got closer, they heard someone shouting.

"What's that?" Evelyn whispered in a
trembling voice.

They were close to the central square
now. Carefully, they peeped around the
corner. A goblin was standing on an
upside-down wooden crate, surrounded

by a crowd of other goblins. They were staring at him with their mouths hanging open.

"And another thing," he was shouting. "I'm not afraid to say that I like playing Guess That Goblin, even though some goblins think it's a children's game. Just because I'm young, that doesn't mean

I'm an idiot. I've got amazing ideas and plans. Jack Frost knows how wonderful and clever I am. You're all going to be sorry for laughing at me for saying the moon is made of green cheese. I can prove it."

"He seems a bit confused," said Evelyn. "Even for a goblin."

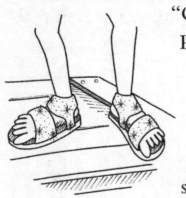

"Oh my goodness," said Rachel. "Look at his feet."

The loud young goblin was wearing sparkly orange sandals and a blue woolly hat.

"He must be the goblin that we saw in the Seeing Pool," said Kirsty. "He's got the pink gemstone."

"Of course," said Evelyn. "That's why he feels so confident in front of all these other goblins. The pink gemstone gives you the courage to speak your mind."

"We can't go up to him now," said Rachel. "All the goblins are staring at him."

But at that moment, the young goblin jumped down from his crate and stomped off down an alleyway.

"We have to follow him," Kirsty whispered. "We'll just have to hope that the other goblins don't see us."

Keeping their fingers crossed, the fairies stayed in the shadows and fluttered along the side of the square.

"There are his footprints," said Rachel, pointing to a set of enormous goblin prints in the snow. "They will lead us straight to him."

The fairies slipped into the tumble-down alleyway. They followed the prints until they reached a hut tucked in between two threadbare fir trees. It was hard to tell if the hut was as shabby as the alleyway, because it was covered in pictures. Rachel spotted several posters for Frosty and the Gobolicious Band. There were leaflets for goblin shops and even recipes with photographs of green-goo cupcakes and sludge sausages.

"I've never seen a goblin hut like this before," said Rachel.

"What now?" asked Kirsty. "As soon as the goblin spots us, he'll throw the magical snowflake."

"We have to get in without being seen," said Evelyn. "But how?"

Chapter Eight
Magical Mice

"There's no way we can get in," said Rachel. "The huts are tiny inside. The goblin would see us straight away. Besides, there's hardly enough room for a mouse to creep in under the door, let alone a fairy."

"Oh!" said Kirsty suddenly. "You've given me an idea. Evelyn, could you turn us into mice? If we were that small, we could creep in under the door."

"Yes, and we should be able to keep out of the goblin's sight," said Evelyn.

Just then, they heard goblin voices at the far end of the alleyway. "They're coming this way," said Rachel. "Hurry." Evelyn raised her wand and whispered a spell.

Ears and tail, small and light,
Good at keeping out of sight.
Change these fairies into mice;
We'll find the gemstone in a trice!

A wisp of sparkling fairy dust spiralled from her wand and rippled from Rachel to Kirsty and then back to Evelyn. As soon as it touched them, they felt fur

tickling their faces.

"My ears are getting bigger," said
Kirsty with a giggle.

She reached up to touch them, and
realised that she had paws instead of
hands.

"We're tiny," said Rachel, looking at
Kirsty and Evelyn. They had all become

small, brown field mice.

"Those goblin voices are getting closer," said Evelyn.

Twitching their whiskers, the three mice scurried under the goblin's door and pressed themselves up against the wall of

the hut.

The young goblin was sitting in front of a feeble fire, rubbing his bony hands together. He had kicked off his orange sandals, but his hat was still perched on top of his knobbly head.

"No silly fairies are going to find my hiding place," he said, squawking with laughter. "I'll be the first goblin ever to beat the fairies and follow Jack Frost's orders. I'll be made chief goblin. I'll get medals. I'll make the others call me sir."

He reached out to a pile of green-goo cupcakes on a little table and shoved one into his mouth.

"They'll never guess I've hidden it in my chimney," he said, spraying green crumbs across the floor. "And even if they do, they're not going to want to singe their weedy wings."

The mice exchanged worried glances.

"The goblin's right," Kirsty whispered. "We can't get into the chimney as mice or as fairies!"

Chapter Nine
Green-Goo Distraction

"I have an idea," said Rachel. "If the goblin thinks that we've guessed his hiding place, he might move the gemstone himself."

"And then we would have a chance to take it back," said Kirsty.

"We have to let him hear us," said
Evelyn.

Rachel and Kirsty looked at her in
surprise.

"Do you mean that you want us to get
caught?" Rachel asked.

"No," said Evelyn. "But what if the
goblin hears fairy voices talking about
his hiding place?"

Rachel and Kirsty ran around the edge
of the hut. Kirsty stopped by the fireplace
and Rachel scurried behind a large,
mouldy marshmallow.

Evelyn put her paws over her mouth to
make it sound as if she was outside.

"He's in here," she called.

The goblin leapt to his feet and pulled
out the magical snowflake.

On the other side of the room, Rachel

said, "We have to get in. He can't catch us all with that magical snowflake."

"They can see me!" the goblin squeaked.

He raced to the door and bolted it shut. Then he ran to the window and shut the curtains.

"Let's fly down the chimney," said Kirsty. "That's a good hiding place."

"Oh no you don't," muttered the goblin.
"I'm cleverer than you."

He sprang towards the fireplace and
reached up inside the chimney. When he
pulled his hand out, he was holding a
small velvet pouch.

"I'll fool them," he whispered.

He dropped the pouch into a cracked glass jar on the mantelpiece. Then he sat down, but he didn't relax. He sat bolt upright, watching the chimney. Rachel and Kirsty ran back around the room to where Evelyn was waiting.

"We have to distract him," said Rachel. "If he sees a fairy, he'll use the magic snowflake."

Kirsty looked at the table where

the green-goo cupcakes were piled up higgledy-piggledy. She smiled, and her whiskers bristled.

"The goblin wouldn't like two little mice nibbling his cakes," she said. "If we can keep him watching us, maybe Evelyn can turn back into a fairy and take the gemstone without him noticing."

"It's risky," said Rachel. "If he turns

around and sees her, he'll send her to the dungeon."

"We won't let him turn around," said Kirsty. "We'll be the strangest, most annoying mice he's ever seen. We just can't let him know that we're fairies."

"Let's try," said Evelyn. "Let's do it for the mermicorns."

Chapter Nine
Back to the Ocean

Rachel and Kirsty scampered around to the back of the goblin's chair. The space between the floor and the chair was just big enough for them to squeeze through. It was dark and dusty under there. They crawled past snoozing spiders and stale cupcake crumbs.

"I see the goblin's legs," Rachel

whispered.

"Go left," said Kirsty. "The table's at the side of the chair."

Side by side, the two mice edged out from underneath the chair. They each chose a table leg.

"How do we climb up?" Kirsty asked.

"I think we just dig our tiny little claws in, and use our tails to balance,"

said Rachel, her whiskers twitching as she smiled. "I'm hoping it comes naturally."

Silently, they climbed up the table legs, going faster and faster. They reached the top at the same time. A mountain of green cakes towered above them.

"Those cakes smell really bad," Rachel whispered.

"Let's each choose one," said Kirsty. "Then we just have to do everything we can to keep him looking at us."

They each pulled a cake towards them, and then Rachel let out a loud *SQUEAK!* The goblin turned to look at her.

"Hey, get off my cakes!" he yelled.

He swiped at the little mouse, but she dodged him and started nibbling.

Before he could try to hit her again,
Kirsty squeaked too.

"Get out of here!" the goblin screeched.
He snatched at the mice, trying to

catch them, but they were too quick
for him. Kirsty and Rachel ran left and
right, leaping over his hand and even
swinging under the table with their tails.
"You squeaky little pests," he yelled.
"Come here!"

In between leaps and swings, Rachel
saw Evelyn fluttering in front of the
mantelpiece. But just
as she reached for
the jar, the goblin
started to turn
around.

SQUEAK!
The mice sprang
through the air
and landed on the
front of the goblin's
woolly hat. Clinging

on with their front paws, they jumped
down and pulled the hat over his eyes.

"Help!" the goblin shrieked. "Mouse
attack! Crazy mice!"

He spun around, trying to swipe at the
dangling mice. Just as he snatched the hat
from his head, Evelyn grabbed the velvet
bag from the jar and waved her wand.

"Fairies!" the goblin shouted.

He flung the
magical snowflake
at Evelyn, just as
she and the mice
disappeared in a
twinkling of fairy
dust.

Rachel and
Kirsty blinked, and
saw that they were
fluttering above the
blue ocean.

"We're fairies again," said Rachel.
"Thank goodness."

Evelyn put her arms around
them, and all three of them
twirled around in the air, laughing.
"That was close," Evelyn said. "It's thanks
to you that I'm safe, and that I have this."

She took the pink gemstone out of the velvet pouch, and it seemed to glow more brightly.

"How will you tell Topaz that you've got it back?" Rachel asked.

"I think she already knows," said Evelyn. "She has a very special

connection with the gems."

She flew down and held the gem in the water. At once, the water began to whirl around, changing from blue to pink. The whirlpool spun faster and deeper. Then a spiral horn rose out of the water.

"Topaz!" cried all the fairies at once.

Evelyn placed the gem back in Topaz's necklace, and then they all put their

arms around the mermicorn's neck. She
nuzzled them gratefully.

"There's one more gem to find," said
Evelyn. "But before we go looking for it,
how about a swim with a mermicorn?"

Rachel and Kirsty exchanged an excited smile.

"Yes please!" they exclaimed.

Story Three
Helping Others

Chapter Eleven
Return to Mermicorn Island

Evelyn, Rachel and Kirsty had fun
diving through the foaming waves with
Topaz, but they didn't play for long. Jack
Frost still had the green gemstone, and
without it none of the fairies would have
the confidence to advise others. Soon,
the three friends were hurrying along a
marble corridor in the Fairyland Palace.

"I'm glad we can give the queen some good news," said Kirsty. "The last time we saw her, the pink gemstone was still missing."

They entered the throne room. Queen Titania was standing beside the window, gazing out over Fairyland. She turned when the fairies came in, and they curtsied. The queen looked worried.

"We found the pink gemstone," said

Rachel. "Now there is just one left to find."

"Thank you," said the queen. "You have been very brave. I wish I knew what to advise you to do next. But now Jack Frost has the green gemstone, I don't feel sure that my advice is wise."

"I'm sorry, Your Majesty," said Evelyn, hanging her head.

The queen came forward and placed one hand on Evelyn's shoulder.

"The only person to blame is Jack Frost," she said.

"Where are the fairies from the

festival?" asked Kirsty, gazing around.
The throne room was empty apart from
one spindly frog footman.

"They have gone back to Mermicorn
Island," said the queen. "I am not sure
why."

"Perhaps we had better go to the island
too," said Rachel.

"Perhaps," said the queen. "I'm not sure.
The only thing I know is that I won't
be able to give advice until the green
gemstone is back where it belongs."

The fairies curtsied, and turned to
leave. At the throne room door, Bertram,
the frog footman, spoke shyly to them.

"Excuse me," he said. "I think I know
why the fairies went back to the island.
It was because of the Amazing Advisor."

"Who's that?" asked Evelyn.

"All I know is that the Amazing Advisor told them everything would be all right if they went back to the island," he said. "He sounded very sure of himself and he gave great advice."

Rachel and Kirsty exchanged a puzzled glance.

"Who could he be?" Kirsty asked.

"I don't know," Rachel replied.
"But I think we should go straight to
Mermicorn Island and find out."

The fairies flew out across the shining
blue sea. The tall, slender trees of
Mermicorn Island were bending in the
warm, gentle breeze.

"The island looks like a green gemstone

in the water," said Kirsty.

The fairies on the golden beach were queuing up outside a blue tipi. It was decorated with white shells, and the sign beside it said:

The Amazing Advisor's Seashell Cave
FREE Advice for Fairies

There were so many fairies crowding

around the entrance that it was impossible to see inside.

"Let's look around the back," Rachel suggested. "Maybe we can find a clue."

They fluttered around and saw that there was a small flap on the other side of the tipi.

"It's just like a back door," said Evelyn.

At that moment, the flap was lifted and two figures stepped out of the tipi. They were wearing long blue capes that reached to the ground, with huge hoods that covered their faces. Each of them was wearing a badge that said 'Amazing Advisor's Helper'. The capes were decorated with the same white shells as the tipi.

They sat down on two driftwood logs. One of the helpers pulled a green bottle

from under his cape. He twisted the lid
and fizzy green bubbles spurted out.

"Yum!" said the other helper, snatching
the bottle and taking a big glug. "I love
cabbage pop."

"What a squawky voice he has," said
Kirsty.

The first helper burped and they both
cackled with laughter.

"And what bad manners," said Evelyn.

"It's too hot on this island," grumbled the first helper. "And I'm fed up with fairies."

He threw back his hood, and Rachel clutched Kirsty's hand.

"Oh no," said Evelyn. "Goblins!"

Chapter Twelve
The Amazing Advisor

The three fairies darted out of sight behind the sand dunes. They peered out from behind a clump of beachgrass. The second goblin was busy complaining.

"Why can't we go home?" he whined. "I'm worried that all the goodness and sweetness is catching."

"I'm sure I'm allergic to fairy dust,"

said the first goblin. "But we can't go home until that mermicorn turns up. Jack Frost won't stop yelling at us until he has her gemstones."

The three fairies exchanged worried glances.

"Come on," said the second goblin, finishing the last drops of cabbage pop. "Maybe the mermicorn will turn up soon. Then we can jump in the boat, catch it and get back to Goblin Grotto."

Putting their hoods up again, they ducked back into the tipi.

"So they've got a boat," said Rachel. "They're planning to catch Topaz."

Evelyn gave a little sniff, and tears glistened in her eyes.

"Don't worry," said Kirsty, putting her arm around Evelyn and giving her a

squeeze. "We won't let them take Topaz. We're one step ahead of them already, because we know their plan. We have to warn the other fairies."

"Let's just see if we can hear anything else," said Rachel.

They fluttered closer and pressed their ears against the tipi. At once they heard a strange, deep voice.

"How can I help you, young fairy?"

"That must be the Amazing Advisor," Kirsty whispered. "I suppose it's another goblin in disguise."

"I want to protect my magical objects from Jack Frost," said a clear, musical voice. "What should I do?"

"Hide them under a plant pot in your garden," boomed the Amazing Advisor. "Next!"

Another fairy voice spoke. "I feel as if all my confidence has been taken away. How can I be the best that I can be?"

"Easy," said the Amazing Advisor. "Confidence isn't about being the best you that you can be. It's about being better than other people. Have a competition with your friends that you know you can win. Next!"

"The Amazing Advisor doesn't sound

very amazing to me," said Rachel. "What awful advice!"

"But he sounds so confident that the fairies are listening to him," said Kirsty, groaning.

"He must have the green gemstone," said Evelyn. "It's giving him the confidence to advise others."

"The Amazing Advisor is taking a

break," squawked one of the goblin advisors. "Come back later."

The back flap of the tipi trembled, and the fairies darted out of sight. A tall figure in a bright-blue cloak stepped out of the tipi, followed by four goblin helpers. He threw back his hood, and the fairies gasped. The Amazing Advisor wasn't another goblin after all. It was Jack Frost himself!

Chapter Thirteen
Going Fishing

"Give me some water," Jack Frost snapped at the goblins. "Using that deep voice is hurting my throat."

While the goblins scurried to obey, Jack Frost touched the green gemstone that hung around his neck.

"The last gemstone," whispered Evelyn.

"From now on, no one can feel better

or more important than me,' said Jack
Frost with a thin smile. "The fairies won't
be able to advise anyone, and I'll take
over in the confusion. Fairyland will be
mine!"

He threw his head back and cackled
with laughter.

"I want to go
home," whined the
tallest goblin.

Jack Frost stopped
cackling and turned
on him with blazing
eyes.

"Go and eavesdrop
on the fairies," he
yelled. "They're
bound to spot the
mermicorn as soon

as it turns up. Then we'll show it this gemstone and it'll follow us anywhere. Go!"

The goblin scurried back into the tipi.

"Soon all the mermicorn magic will belong to me," said Jack Frost. "I've heard mermicorns can time-travel, grant wishes and cure illness."

"Those are just legends," Evelyn muttered. "Topaz can't do those things. But if Jack Frost gets the gemstones again he will be more powerful than ever."

"He'll be cross when he finds out that Topaz can't do what he wants," said Kirsty.

"We have to stop him," said Rachel. "Luckily the island is full of fairies. Let's go and tell them who the Amazing Advisor really is."

But before they could move, the tallest goblin came tumbling out of the tipi.

"It's back!" he squealed. "One of the fairies said she saw a horn in the water."

"At last!" said Jack Frost, throwing off his cloak. "The boat is on the other side of the island. Go!"

The goblins sprinted off and Jack Frost

disappeared in a flash of blue lightning.

"There's no time to tell the other fairies," said Evelyn. "We have to save Topaz!"

Rachel, Kirsty and Evelyn zoomed across the island. They flew over the goblins below and soon reached the other side of the little island. A little ice-blue fishing trawler was bobbing on the water. Jack Frost was in the cabin.

"Let's hide behind the boat," said Kirsty.

"The goblins will be here any minute."

They ducked down at the back of the boat just in time. The goblins burst out of a clump of trees and clambered on board.

"Get this boat moving!" Jack Frost roared. "Go round to where the mermicorn was seen. Faster!"

Soon the boat was chugging around

the island. The fairies clung on to the
back, keeping their heads down.

"We have to get the gemstone back
before Topaz sees it," said Evelyn.
"Otherwise I won't be able to stop him
from following the boat."

They peeped over the side and saw Jack
Frost put the gemstone
in a bottle and cork
it up. He tied one
end of a rope around
the bottle. Then he
threw the bottle over
the back of the boat
and dragged it along
behind them, holding
on to the rope.

"Now all we have
to do is wait for the

mermicorn to spot it," he said. "When the mermicorn follows it, we'll lead it into deeper water and capture it – and all its other magical gemstones too."

Chapter Fourteen
Magical Bubbles

The fairies exchanged worried glances.

"We can't go and untie the rope with Jack Frost watching," said Kirsty.

"We'd be spotted at once if we flew over and pulled the bottle out of the water," said Evelyn.

"We have to get to the bottle from underneath," said Rachel. "That's the only way to reach it without being spotted. Then we can uncork the bottle and save the gemstone."

"But we can't swim underwater for long without coming up for air, and the boat is going quite fast," said Evelyn. "Jack Frost will see us."

The boat chugged along, and spray flew into the fairies' eyes. Suddenly, Kirsty had an idea.

"Rachel, do you remember our adventure with Shannon the Ocean Fairy?" she asked. "If Evelyn could put magical bubbles on our heads, we could breathe underwater."

"Yes, I know Shannon's bubbles spell," said Evelyn. "I can do it, but my magic works differently from hers. The bubbles won't be strong enough for you to dive very deep. You will have to stay near the surface."

"That's OK," said Rachel. "We don't need to dive down far to get the bottle."

Each of them took a deep breath and dived underwater. Three shiny bubbles floated out of Evelyn's wand and settled over their heads. There was a *POP* as the bubbles disappeared.

"We can breathe," said Rachel.

"But the boat is getting away," said Kirsty.

Evelyn pointed her wand at the water behind them, and it started to bubble and churn. Then, *WHOOSH!* The water pushed them forwards until they were just below the bottle.

"I've got it!" cried Rachel, slipping the bottle out of the rope.

But in her excitement, she lifted her head and it broke the surface of the water. Jack Frost spotted her at once.

"Fairies!" he shrieked. "Goblins, get them!"

The engine stopped and there were four splashes as the goblins belly-flopped into the water.

"Uncork it!" cried Kirsty.

But a bony green hand wrenched the bottle away from Rachel. The goblin cackled and rattled the gemstone under Rachel's nose.

"Give it back," said Kirsty. "It doesn't belong to you."

"It does now," said the goblin, pulling a face at her.

He threw the bottle to another goblin, but Evelyn rose out of the water and caught it. The third goblin snatched at her wings and pulled her backwards, and the bottle flew out of her hand.

"Butterfingers," squawked the fourth goblin. "Hey, watch this!"

He balanced the bottle on his head. At that moment, a whirlpool of colour

appeared behind him. A spiral horn broke through the water.

"Topaz!" cried Kirsty in delight.

Topaz whinnied loudly and made the goblin jump. The precious bottle fell off his head … and sank beneath the waves. "The gemstone!" cried Evelyn.

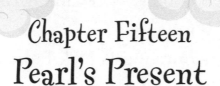

Chapter Fifteen
Pearl's Present

"No!" Jack Frost roared.

Rachel and Kirsty dived after the bottle. It was already far below, turning over and over as it sank. They tried to follow it, but there was a loud *POP* and their bubbles burst. Holding their breath, they swam back to the surface. The green gemstone disappeared into the darkness.

When Rachel and Kirsty reached the surface, the goblins were clambering back on to the boat.

"You nincompoops!" Jack Frost was yelling at them. "Fuzz for brains! Get this boat moving and don't you dare drip on me!"

He whirled around and glared at Topaz

and the fairies. They trod water, staring
up at him.

"At least you've lost the gemstone,
too," he hissed. "No fairy will ever feel
confident about giving advice again."

The trawler chugged away towards the
shore. The roar of the engine faded.

"I'm so sorry, Evelyn," said Rachel,
turning to the Mermicorn Fairy with
tears in her eyes. "We've let you down."

"It wasn't your fault," said Evelyn. "Oh,
Topaz, I'm sorry."

The mermicorn hung her head and the
fairies wrapped their arms around her.

SPLASH!

A large, silvery tail had risen out of the
water. Rainbow colours danced across it.
With another splash, the tail disappeared.
Then a head rose out of the water. Blue

eyes twinkled at them, and long blonde hair fanned out upon the waves.

"It's a mermaid," said Rachel in a whispery voice.

The mermaid smiled.

"My name is Pearl," she said. "I couldn't resist meeting the only two humans to have travelled to Fairyland."

"It's incredible to meet you," said Kirsty.

"I was just waiting for Jack Frost to leave before I gave you this," Pearl said to Evelyn. "It landed beside me as I was pruning the seaweed."

She lifted her hand out of the water, holding the precious bottle. The green gemstone glowed inside it. Evelyn let out a cry of delight. In a trice, the gemstone was out of the bottle and back around

Topaz's neck.

"Thank you, Pearl," said Kirsty. "You've saved the day!"

Pearl smiled again. Then, with a flick of her shining tail, she was gone.

"I can't wait to tell the others the good news," said Evelyn. "Rachel and Kirsty, how can I ever thank you? Without you there would be no Mermicorn Festival and no confident fairies."

"It really was a wonderful watery adventure," said Rachel.

Evelyn hugged them both, and Topaz dipped her horn into the water. The waves changed colour around them, shifting between the colours of the rainbow.

"That's her way of saying thank you," said Evelyn.

Rachel and Kirsty buried their faces
in the mermicorn's beautiful mane. It
was soft and warm, and it smelled like
jasmine. Suddenly, everything started to
spin around. Laughing and dizzy, the girls
looked up and saw that they were back
in Rachel's sitting room. The fire was
crackling in the grate, and the rain was
still beating on the window.

"Here we are," said Mr Walker, coming
in with a tray. "Two hot chocolates with

whipped cream and sprinkles."

Rachel and Kirsty shared a happy smile. As usual, no time had passed while they had been away.

"That's one of the things I love about Fairyland," said Kirsty. "Even after the most incredible adventure, there's still a whole week of summer holidays ahead of us."

"As well as two mugs of the best hot chocolate in the world," said Rachel. "Yum!"

The End

Now it's time for Kirsty and
Rachel to help...

Etta the Elephant Fairy

Read on for a sneak peek ...

Rachel Walker gazed out of the car
window as they turned into the gates of
Tail and Trunk Safari Park, on the edge
of Wetherbury Village. "Wow, I can't
believe we're here!"

"I'm so glad we entered the
competition," Kirsty Tate said, sitting
beside her friend.

At school, Rachel had made a collage
of all the endangered animals in the
world, including tigers and pandas and
even a tiny Amazonian frog. Rachel's

teacher had entered her collage for a picture competition run by the safari park – and she'd won!

The prize was a trip to the park, with Rachel's parents. They were going to learn all about how to help animals and save them from danger. Best of all, they were booked to stay in a cabin overnight!

The car bumped down the drive, past a gift shop and into the park.

"There's the monkey enclosure!" Rachel said, pointing towards a cluster of trees where monkeys swung by their long tails.

"And that's the Giraffe Junction," Kirsty said, gazing up and up and up at the long neck of a giraffe chewing leaves. The giraffe flicked an ear at them and they laughed with delight.

"And this looks like our home for

the night," said Mrs Walker, as they pulled up outside a cabin. There were red and white gingham curtains at the windows and a banner above the door that read 'WELCOME, RACHEL AND KIRSTY'! The girls shared an excited glance as they clambered out of the car.

The park manager was standing in front of the cabin, waiting for them. "I'm Ahmed," he said, reaching out to shake their hands. "If you leave your bags here, I'll show you round the rest of the park."

Kirsty and Rachel handed over their bags to Mr and Mrs Walker, who grinned. "We'll unpack. You girls go and have fun. Report back on all the animals!"

Ahmed led the girls over to a truck painted in tiger stripes of orange and black, with big wheels and orange hubs.

"I've worked here all my life," he told them, gazing proudly across the grassland. "You're in for a treat!"

Kirsty and Rachel clambered into the back seat and Ahmed switched the engine on. "Ready?"

"Ready!" Rachel and Kirsty replied, clapping their hands together in delight.

The safari park was HUGE. Ahmed turned the truck through a gate and drove slowly past a big, open lake that glittered in the sunshine.

Honk! HONK!

"What's that noise?" Rachel asked, looking round.

Kirsty spotted a pair of wet, shiny noses poking above the surface of the water. "Seals!" she said.

The truck entered a copse of trees and bamboo, and the girls saw a panda lazing in a branch, chewing a twig. His soft, black eyes watched them as they drove past.

"I love pandas!"Rachel whispered.

"And there – look." Kirsty pointed at a huge rhinoceros that was bathing in a puddle of mud. He lazily scratched one ear on a tree stump.

"The mud keeps him cool in the sun," Ahmed said. "Did you know that the word 'rhinoceros' means 'nose horn'?"

"No, we didn't," Rachel and Kirsty said, smiling at each other. Ahmed told them all about how many species of rhinos there were, and that they could grow to over four metres long. He definitely loved his animal facts.

There was so much to see! Eventually, the truck arrived back at their cabin.

"Would you like to visit the Elephant

Bath later?" Ahmed asked, turning round from the driver's seat. "The elephants are sleeping now but they'll come out at dusk, when it's cooler."

"Yes, please!" the girls said together.

"We can go after supper," Ahmed said, and drove off in a cloud of dust.

Rachel and Kirsty waved goodbye, then ran into the cabin.

Read **Etta the Elephant Fairy** to find out
what adventures are in store for Kirsty and Rachel!

Calling all parents, carers and teachers!
The Rainbow Magic fairies are here to help
your child enter the magical world of reading.
Whatever reading stage they are at, there's
a Rainbow Magic book for everyone!
Here is Lydia the Reading Fairy's guide to
supporting your child's journey at all levels.

Starting Out

1 Our Rainbow Magic Beginner Readers are perfect for first-time readers who are just beginning to develop reading skills and confidence. Approved by teachers, they contain a full range of educational levelling, as well as lively full-colour illustrations.

Developing Readers

2 Rainbow Magic Early Readers contain longer stories and wider vocabulary for building stamina and growing confidence. These are adaptations of our most popular Rainbow Magic stories, specially developed for younger readers in conjunction with an Early Years reading consultant, with full-colour illustrations.

Going Solo

3 The Rainbow Magic chapter books - a mixture of series and one-off specials - contain accessible writing to encourage your child to venture into reading independently. These highly collectible and much-loved magical stories inspire a love of reading to last a lifetime.

www.rainbowmagicbooks.co.uk

"Rainbow Magic got my daughter reading chapter books. Great sparkly covers, cute fairies and traditional stories full of magic that she found impossible to put down" - Mother of Edie (6 years)

"Florence LOVES the Rainbow Magic books. She really enjoys reading now" - Mother of Florence (6 years)

The Rainbow Magic Reading Challenge

Well done, fairy friend – you have completed the book!
This book was worth 10 points.

See how far you have climbed on the
Reading Rainbow opposite.

The more books you read, the more points you will get,
and the closer you will be to becoming a Fairy Princess!

Do you want your own Reading Rainbow?
1. Cut out the coin below
2. Go to the Rainbow Magic website
3. Download and print out your poster
4. Add your coin and climb up the Reading Rainbow!

There's all this and lots more at
www.rainbowmagicbooks.co.uk

You'll find activities, competitions, stories, a special
newsletter and complete profiles of all the
Rainbow Magic fairies. Find a fairy with your name!